Clifford THE BIG RED DOG®

THE BIG ITCH

Adapted by Alison Inches
From the television script "An Itchy Patch"
by Anne-Marie Perrotta and Tean Schultz
Illustrated by Robbin Cuddy

Based on the Scholastic book series
"Clifford The Big Red Dog"
by Norman Bridwell

ISBN 0-439-44943-X

10 9 8 7 6 5 4 3 2 1   03 04 05 06 07

Printed in the U.S.A.
First printing, September 2003

SCHOLASTIC INC.
New York   Toronto   London   Auckland   Sydney
Mexico City   New Delhi   Hong Kong   Buenos Aires

One day Clifford had a big itch.

He scratched it against everything.

He scratched it against an apple tree.

"Clifford!" said Samuel and Ms. Lee.

He scratched it against a stoplight.

"Clifford!" said the bus driver.

He scratched it against Mr. Carson's truck.

"Clifford!" said Mr. Carson.

At home, Clifford scratched . . .

and scratched . . .

and scratched!

"If he keeps scratching," said

Emily Elizabeth's dad,

"he will have to go to the vet."

The vet? thought Clifford.

Clifford had never been to the

new vet before.

Clifford ran to the beach

and told his friends.

"Trust me," said Cleo,

"you do *not* want to go to the vet."

"What should I do?" asked Clifford.

"Stop scratching," said Cleo. "No

scratching—no vet!"

At the library, Clifford tried not

to scratch.

But he was *so* itchy!

He rolled over and over.

Ms. Lee looked out the window.

"Wow," she said.

"Clifford sure has a big itch."

"Clifford!" cried Emily.

"Are you scratching again?"

Clifford pretended to play.

So did Cleo and T-Bone.

"You were just playing?"

Emily Elizabeth asked.

"Woof!" they barked together.

Emily Elizabeth had lunch at Samuel's
Fish and Chips.

"How is Clifford's itch?" asked Samuel.

"I haven't seen him scratch all day," said
Emily Elizabeth.

They looked out at Clifford.

He looked happy.

And he *was* happy.

Cleo and T-Bone were scratching his back!

That feels so good!" said Clifford.

But soon Cleo and T-Bone got tired of scratching.

Clifford's big itch got bigger and bigger!

Clifford ran down the beach.

He jumped into the water.

He rubbed his back on the ferry dock.

"Clifford!" cried Emily Elizabeth.

Clifford looked up.

"It's time to go to the vet," she said.

"Dr. Dihn will take care of you."

Clifford whined.

"It will be okay, " said Emily Elizabeth.

"You'll see."

The whole family drove to the vet.

"You must be Clifford!" said Dr. Dihn.

She checked his back.

"I have some cream that will fix that
rash," said Dr. Dihn.

"Poor Clifford. He's all alone
at the vet's office," said Cleo.

"He's not alone," said T-Bone.

"Emily Elizabeth is with him.

And she would never let anyone hurt him."

Dr. Dihn spread the cream on
Clifford's back.

Clifford felt all better.

He howled with joy.

Everyone cheered for Clifford.

Clifford wagged his tail.

He gave Dr. Dihn a big kiss.

"Oh, my!" she said.

"I think you've made a friend

for life!" Emily Elizabeth said.

"Dr. Dihn took good care of you," said

Emily Elizabeth.

"And I will always take good care of you.

Because you are Clifford, my Big Red Dog!"

Do You Remember?

Circle the right answer.

1. Where was Clifford's itch?
   a. On his head.
   b. On his back.
   c. On his tummy.

2. At the beach, what did Clifford scratch against?
   a. The ferry dock.
   b. A rowboat.
   c. A beach chair.

Which happened first?
Which happened next?
Which happened last?

Write a 1, 2, or 3 in the space after each sentence.

Clifford scratched against Mr. Carson's truck. __2__

Clifford went to the library with Emily. __3__

Clifford scratched against an apple tree. __1__

Answers:

Clifford scratched against an apple tree. (1)
Clifford went to the library with Emily. (3)
Clifford scratched against Mr. Carson's truck. (2)
2. a
1. b